# STAR WARS
## THE LAST JEDI
™

### By Elizabeth Schaefer
### Illustrated by Alan Batson

 A GOLDEN BOOK • NEW YORK

© & ™ 2018 LUCASFILM LTD. All rights reserved. Published in the United States by Golden Books, an imprint of Random House Children's Books, a division of Penguin Random House LLC, 1745 Broadway, New York, NY 10019, and in Canada by Penguin Random House Canada Limited, Toronto. Golden Books, A Golden Book, A Little Golden Book, the G colophon, and the distinctive gold spine are registered trademarks of Penguin Random House LLC.

rhcbooks.com

ISBN 978-0-7364-3586-4 (trade) — ISBN 978-0-7364-3584-0 (ebook)

Printed in the United States of America

10 9 8 7 6 5 4 3 2 1

# A long time ago in a galaxy far, far away . . .

The evil First Order was taking over the galaxy! The brave Resistance tried to stop them, but First Order star destroyers had the heroes on the run! The daring pilot **Poe Dameron** and his squadron of X-wing fighters defended the Resistance fleet, allowing them to escape into hyperspace.

Meanwhile, **General Leia** had sent a young hero named **Rey** on a special mission to the distant planet of Ahch-To to find Leia's brother, **Luke Skywalker**. Luke was the last Jedi— a master of a powerful energy field called the Force. Leia hoped Luke would help defeat the First Order once and for all.

Just when it seemed that the Resistance was safe, the First Order **found them**! The villains had a special machine that could track the Resistance anywhere. As long as the machine existed, the Resistance would never be safe.

General Leia's son, **Kylo Ren**, led the First Order
attack on the Resistance fleet. Kylo was once a student of
Jedi Master Luke Skywalker. But the Supreme Leader of
the First Order—**Snoke**—had turned Kylo Ren to evil.

The Resistance hero **Finn** used to be a stormtrooper and hated the First Order. But Finn was worried about his friend Rey, so he decided to leave the battle to find her.

When Finn tried to board an escape pod, a technician named **Rose** zapped him with an electro-shock prod! She told Finn that Rey could take care of herself. The Resistance needed him!

Together, Rose and Finn
came up with a plan to stop the
First Order's tracking machine. But
the machine was on the **biggest** and
most **dangerous** ship in the First Order
fleet. They needed help to get past the
security systems.

The two heroes blasted off to the
beautiful city of Canto Bight to find the
Master Codebreaker to help them.
Poe Dameron's droid, BB-8,
decided to help, too!

Meanwhile, Rey's mission was not going well. Luke refused to help the Resistance. He wouldn't train Rey in the Force!

Rey's friend and copilot **Chewbacca** made himself at home on the island, though. The Wookiee even made some new friends!

But everything changed when Luke's droid **R2-D2** showed him an old hologram of Leia asking for help.

Luke might not have listened to Rey, but he couldn't ignore his own sister. So Luke agreed to teach Rey.

Rey began training every day with Luke. But as Rey grew stronger, she started connecting with Kylo Ren across the galaxy through **the Force**! Rey began to wonder if she could save Kylo from the dark side.

At Canto Bight, Rose and Finn had crashed their ship on a beach, and the police threw them in jail before they could find the **Master Codebreaker**! But inside their cell, the two heroes met a strange man named **DJ** who helped them escape.

Rose and Finn jumped onto a speedy creature called a **fathier** and raced through the city away from the police, until they reached a cliff! Rose and Finn were stuck!

ZOOOOOOOOM!

DJ and BB-8 had arrived in a ship to rescue Rose and Finn! DJ said he could sneak them into the First Order's main ship—for a price.

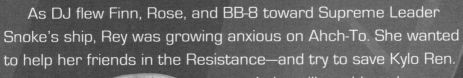

As DJ flew Finn, Rose, and BB-8 toward Supreme Leader Snoke's ship, Rey was growing anxious on Ahch-To. She wanted to help her friends in the Resistance—and try to save Kylo Ren. Luke still would not leave the island, so Rey climbed aboard the *Millennium Falcon* with Chewbacca and R2-D2 and flew away.

Kylo Ren was waiting for Rey on the First Order's ship. She told him to leave the First Order and join the Resistance. But Kylo told Rey that he thought she would be turned to the dark side! He brought Rey before his evil master.

**"Come closer, child,"** Snoke snarled, pulling Rey toward him with the Force.

Meanwhile, DJ had helped Finn, Rose, and BB-8 sneak onto Snoke's ship. But before the heroes could disable the tracking machine, they were discovered by Captain Phasma and her stormtroopers!

DJ cut a deal to escape, but the stormtroopers captured
Finn and Rose. Just when it seemed that the heroes were
doomed, a big **AT-ST walker** started firing all around the
ship. BB-8 had taken control of the walker to save his friends.

Finn grabbed an electrostaff and fought off the stormtroopers. He even **defeated** his old commander, Captain Phasma!

Then Finn, Rose, and BB-8 jumped into a First Order shuttle and **blasted off** to freedom.

Not far away, Kylo Ren watched Snoke
hurting Rey. Kylo knew he had to do something.
So he destroyed his evil master!

Kylo and Rey even worked together to
**defeat** Snoke's powerful red guards.

But instead of joining the Resistance, Kylo
asked Rey to join the First Order—and help him
**take over the galaxy**!

Rey knew that she and Kylo would never be on
the same side. So she took off with Chewbacca
on the *Falcon* to find the Resistance. . . .

Meanwhile, Finn, Rose, and BB-8 had rejoined the Resistance on the planet of Crait. The heroes were hiding in an abandoned base in a big cave.

But soon Kylo Ren and the First Order arrived with gigantic **AT-M6 walkers**. Poe, Finn, Rose, and a small group of Resistance fighters tried to defend the base in old ski speeders. But they were outnumbered and overpowered.

Luckily, Rey and Chewbacca arrived in the *Millennium Falcon* just in time, **blasting** First Order TIE fighters!
But the First Order was too strong, and the Resistance had to retreat into the cave.

When all hope seemed lost, a robed figure
appeared. **Luke Skywalker** had returned to help
the Resistance! Rey's determination and bravery had
inspired him to join the fight.

Kylo was **furious**! He drew his lightsaber and
charged onto the battlefield to destroy his old teacher.

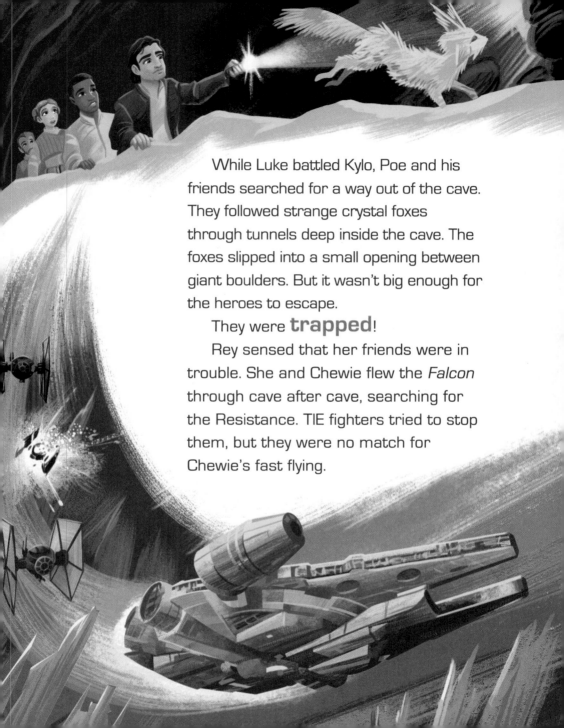

While Luke battled Kylo, Poe and his friends searched for a way out of the cave. They followed strange crystal foxes through tunnels deep inside the cave. The foxes slipped into a small opening between giant boulders. But it wasn't big enough for the heroes to escape.

They were **trapped**!

Rey sensed that her friends were in trouble. She and Chewie flew the *Falcon* through cave after cave, searching for the Resistance. TIE fighters tried to stop them, but they were no match for Chewie's fast flying.

Chewbacca and Rey landed the *Falcon* outside the cave. They quickly found their friends trapped behind the boulders. Rey used **the Force** to lift the enormous rocks blocking their escape. Everyone was free!

Suddenly, during his duel with Kylo, Luke **vanished**! The Jedi Master had never left Ahch-To island. He had used the Force to project an image of himself on Crait to distract Kylo so the Resistance could escape!

But Luke had used up all of his energy to save the Resistance, and so he became **one with the Force** and was at peace.

Soon all of the heroes were blasting off in the *Falcon* to safety. Rey asked Leia how the Resistance could possibly defeat the First Order now.

**"We have everything we need,"** Leia said, gesturing to all of their friends surrounding them.

Rey knew Leia was right. As long as the heroes had **hope**, they could bring peace to the galaxy—together.